First published in the United States 1990 by Chronicle Books.
Copyright © 1988 by Ravensburger Buchverlag Otto Maier GmbH, West Germany
All rights reserved.
Printed in Hong Kong.

Editor's Note: Younger children should only undertake these projects under adult supervision. Parents and teachers should match crafts to the appropriate skill level of the child.

Library of Congress Cataloging-in-Publication Data

Lohf, Sabine.
   [Ich mach was mit Kork. English]
   Things I can make with corks / Sabine Lohf
        p.   cm.
   Translation of: Ich mach was mit Kork.
   Summary: Provides instructions for making castles, games, animals, and other projects out of corks.
   ISBN: 0-87701-726-3
   1. Cork craft—Juvenile literature.   [1. Cork craft.   2. Handicraft.]   I. Title
TT190.5.L64 1990
745.51—dc20   89-22358
                                                                                      CIP
                                                                                       AC

10 9 8 7 6 5 4 3 2 1

Chronicle Books
275 Fifth Street
San Francisco, California 94103

Things I Can Make with
CORKS

Sabine Lohf

You can make all these things with corks.

Chronicle Books • San Francisco

Cork Castles

A Zoo

Hello, up there!

A Desert Oasis

Cat and Mouse Game

Rules for playing:

Each player places a mouse on the board and holds the mouse by its tail. When the cat (a player who tries to cover the mice with a bowl) appears, the mice are quickly pulled back, away from the circle. The mice that get trapped are out of the game. The player whose mouse stays on the board the longest is the winner and gets to be the cat in the next round.

Look out!
Here comes the cat!

Floating Animals

Cut out a paper figure and stick it into a cork that's been cut in half.

Is there room for one more?

Parachutists

The parachute is rolled up like this before it is thrown high into the air.

Horses and Indians

Flying Elf Game

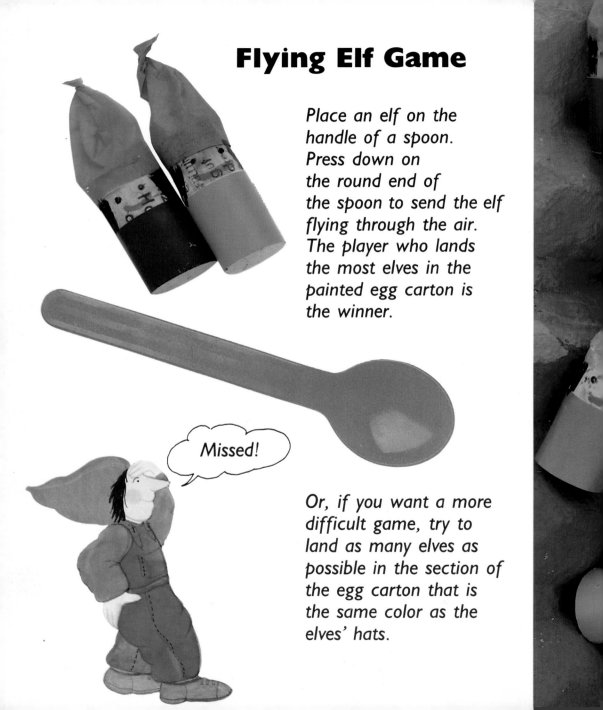

Place an elf on the handle of a spoon. Press down on the round end of the spoon to send the elf flying through the air. The player who lands the most elves in the painted egg carton is the winner.

Missed!

Or, if you want a more difficult game, try to land as many elves as possible in the section of the egg carton that is the same color as the elves' hats.

Ink Stamps

Press the corks into
an ink pad or into real
paints. You can make
all kinds of colorful
pictures.

Almost finished.

A Cork Family